Copyright © 2019 by Hachette Book Group
Published in association with JellyTelly Press

Cover copyright © 2019 by Hachette Book Group
Text copyright © 2019 Phil Vischer Enterprises, Inc.

JellyTelly Press is a division of JellyTelly, LLC.

FaithWords is a division of Hachette Book Group, Inc. The FaithWords name and logo are trademarks of Hachette Book Group, Inc.

FaithWords
Hachette Book Group
1290 Avenue of the Americas, New York, NY 10104

hachettebookgroup.com | faithwords.com | jellytelly.com

Buck Denver and Friends created by Phil Vischer. *Buck Denver Asks®.. What's in the Bible?* trademark and character rights are owned by Phil Vischer IP, LLC and used by permission under license from Jellyfish One, LLC.

Written by Phil Vischer
Illustrated by Greg Hardin and Kenny Yamada

Art Direction and Design: John Trent
Creative Direction: Phil Vischer and Anne Fogerty

First Edition: March 2019

Scripture quotations are from the ESV® Bible (The Holy Bible, English Standard Version®), copyright © 2001 by Crossway, a publishing ministry of Good News Publishers. Used by permission. All rights reserved.

Library of Congress Cataloging-in-Publication Data has been applied for.

10 9 8 7 6 5 4 3 2 1
ISBN: 978-1-5460-1191-0
Printed in China
APS

Buck Denver's
Hammer of STRENGTH

A Lesson in LOVING OTHERS

Written by Phil Vischer
Illustrated by Greg Hardin & Kenny Yamada

SMASH!

A loud noise knocked Marcy backward into the cotton candy machine. Big bundles of cotton candy fell all over her!

"What was that noise?" she asked.

Sunday School Lady and Marcy were setting up for the church carnival. They had snacks and games—everything you'd want for a super fun day!

"Let's see what happened,"
said Sunday School Lady.

When they got to the street, they couldn't believe their eyes.

The front window of Chuck Waggin's Cowboy Store was smashed to bits! And standing in front of the broken window was their friend Buck Denver.

"Buck!" Marcy yelled. "Are you okay? What happened to the window?"

CHUCK WAGGIN'S COWBOY STORE

Chuck Waggin ran outside. "My window!" he shouted.

Buck looked very unhappy.

"It was an accident," he mumbled.

"What happened, Buck?" asked Sunday School Lady.
"How did you break that big window?"

Buck moved to the side. Behind him was a very, VERY big hammer.

Chuck Waggin couldn't believe it.
"You hit my window with a giant hammer?"

"It was an accident!" Buck said. "It's my Super Hammer of Strength! I was carrying it around to show everyone how strong I am! I was trying to hold it up over my head. But it's HEAVY! I lost my balance, and the hammer fell right through Chuck's window."

Buck Denver looked very sad. "I guess I'm not as strong as I thought."

Sunday School Lady put her hand on Buck's shoulder.

"You don't need a hammer to show how strong you are, Buck. You need **LOVE!**"

Buck Denver was confused.

"Love? You mean hugs and kisses? Or, mushy, gushy greeting cards with hearts and frilly stuff? What does all that have to do with being strong?"

"If that's what you think love is, Buck," said Chuck Waggin, "you don't know REAL love!"

Marcy had an idea. "Is there a story we could tell about real love?" she asked.

Sunday School Lady grabbed her flannelgraph. It wasn't an ordinary flannelgraph, of course. It was a MAGIC flannelgraph.

"Chuck Waggin, do you know a story about real love?" she asked.

"I sure do!" he replied. "Just tap on that ol' flannelgraph, and we'll tell a tale!"

Sunday School Lady tapped on the Magic Flannelgraph ...

… and suddenly the four friends weren't standing NEXT to the flannelgraph, they were IN the flannelgraph!

Chuck Waggin rubbed his arms.

"I can never get used to this!" he said. "Everything's fuzzy in here! Like a sheep right after a haircut!"

"What's our story?" Buck asked.

"Ah, yes! See that fella over there?" Chuck Waggin pointed to a man lying on the ground. He was covered with scrapes and bruises.

"What happened? Did he fall off his bike?" Buck asked.

"Nope," replied Chuck Waggin. "We're in Israel, a long, long time ago. Before bikes were invented! This poor guy was just beaten up by some real bad dudes! They took his money, took his donkey—took everything—and just left him there on the side of the road!"

Chuck turned to Buck Denver. "Will anyone show him love? And what will that love look like?"

A man came along wearing very fancy clothes. He was a priest of Israel. He worked in God's temple every day. Surely he would help the man.

"Let's see what this fellow does," said Chuck.

But the priest looked at the man, then kept right on walking!

Buck was surprised. "He didn't even give him a get-well card! Or a hug! Or anything!"

"Wait," Marcy said, "here comes another guy!"

It was another man from Israel. A Levite, who helped out in the temple. Surely he would help the man.

"Let's see what this fellow does," said Chuck.

But just like the priest, the Levite took one look at the hurt man and walked right past him.

"That's not very nice!" Buck yelled. "I don't know if he needs hugs and kisses and cards, but someone should at least HELP this guy!"

One more man came riding down the path. He didn't look like the others.

"He's not from Israel," said Chuck Waggin. "He's from Samaria. People from Samaria and people from Israel didn't like each other at all."

"There's no way he's going to help him!" Buck muttered.

But Buck was wrong. The Samaritan got down from his donkey and ran to the hurt man. He wrapped bandages around his bruises and cuts. He lifted him up onto his donkey and walked beside him all the way to an inn.

The man from Samaria gave the innkeeper money and said, "Take care of my friend. If this isn't enough, I will come back and pay more."

Buck's eyes were wide.

"Wow! Is that what love looks like?"

Sunday School Lady smiled. "That's love, Buck!
The Bible says love puts other people first."

"That's right," Chuck Waggin added. "The Samaritan man
gave up a lot to help his enemy. It takes great strength to give
up so much for someone else. Jesus told this story so we'd
know what real love looks like."

"And no one knows real love better than Jesus!
We have one more story to tell," Sunday School
Lady said as she tapped the ground.

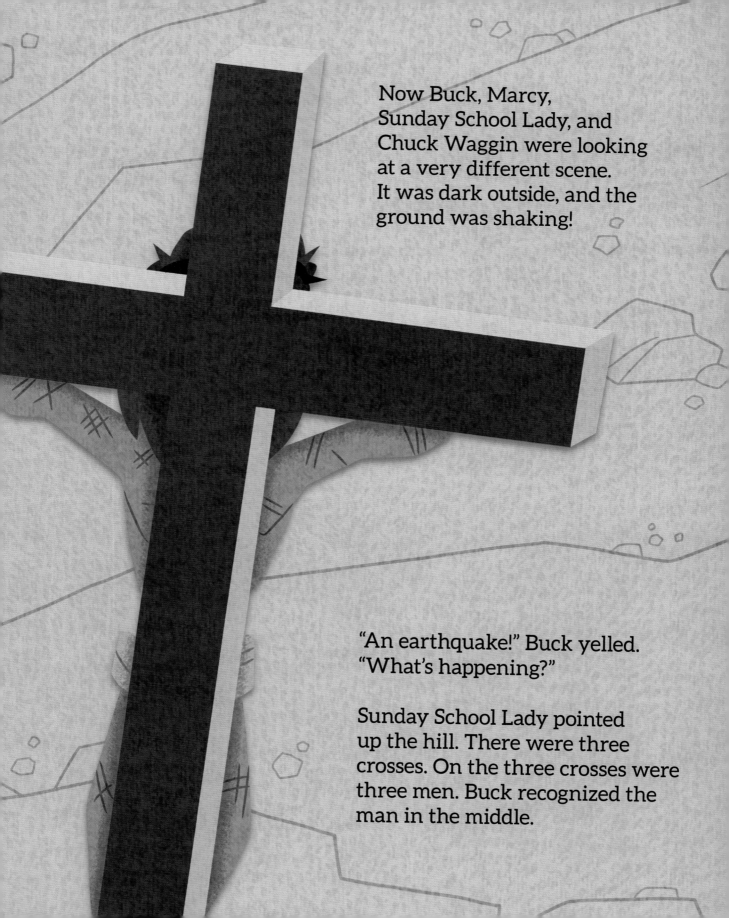

Now Buck, Marcy, Sunday School Lady, and Chuck Waggin were looking at a very different scene. It was dark outside, and the ground was shaking!

"An earthquake!" Buck yelled. "What's happening?"

Sunday School Lady pointed up the hill. There were three crosses. On the three crosses were three men. Buck recognized the man in the middle.

"That's Jesus," he said.
"He's on the cross. Is He dying?"

"Yes, He is, Buck,"
Sunday School Lady answered.

"But why? Why did He
have to die?" Buck asked.

"He didn't HAVE to die.
He CHOSE to die. For us.
Do you remember what
'sin' is?" she asked.

"Sure," Buck answered. "Sin is when we put ourselves first. When we say, 'I don't want to do things Your way, God, I want to do things MY way.'"

"That's right," said Sunday School Lady, looking sad. "Sin keeps us away from God. We can't be God's friends when we sin. Unless someone takes our sin away, we'll be apart from God forever."

Buck was still confused.

"But what does all this have to do with Jesus?"

"That's the amazing part of the story, Buck. Jesus took all of our sin and put it on Himself. He died with all of our sin on Him, so we wouldn't have to. So we could be with God!"

Buck couldn't believe what he was hearing.

"Wow. Is that love?"

Sunday School Lady smiled.

"That's love. The biggest love of all time. The Good Samaritan gave his time and his money to show love to the man who'd been beaten up and robbed. But Jesus gave much more than His time and money. Jesus gave His life. For us."

Buck thought about that.

"So, we're like the man who needed help. We were alone and hurting. And Jesus gave up everything to help us. Not just His money and His time ... but His whole life."

Just then Marcy spoke up. "That kind of love isn't mushy gushy at all! That kind of love takes strength!"

"Super strength!" Buck yelled.

Then Buck got sad.

"But Jesus died. Does that mean we'll never see Him again?"

"No, Buck." Now Sunday School Lady was smiling BIG. "Jesus is SO strong, even DEATH couldn't beat Him! Jesus was dead for three days, then ... BOOM! He beat sin. He beat death. He came back to life!"

"He's the ultimate superhero!" Buck yelled. "I want to be strong like that! I want to show love like the Good Samaritan did! Like Jesus did! I don't need a hammer—I need love!"

"And love won't smash my front window!" Chuck Waggin laughed.

Sunday School Lady
tapped the ground again ...

... and everyone was back outside Chuck's store.

Buck looked at his big hammer.

"I used to think a giant hammer would make me strong, and that love was just hugs and kisses," he said. "Now I know real love is the strongest thing of all!"

Everyone smiled.

Chuck Waggin looked at his broken window.

"I guess the first way I can show love," Buck said,
"is by helping you clean up your window!"

Chuck smiled. "But what do we do with that big ol' hammer?"

Marcy had an idea. "I think we could use it in our carnival!"

DING!

Family Connection

Help your family **KNOW** the love of God,
GROW in God's love, and **SHOW** God's love to others.

CONNECT after reading:

ASK:

1. Why was Buck carrying around a big hammer?
2. What happened when Buck tried to show love through physical strength?
3. Why do you think the Samaritan showed great strength through loving the hurt man?
4. What makes Jesus' love the most powerful love of all?
5. What are some ways we can love others with God's strong love?

READ:

- Read the story of the Good Samaritan in Luke 10:25-37.
- Discover God's powerful love through the story of Calvary and the Resurrection in Matthew 27:32-28:20.

REMEMBER:

Real love puts others first, which shows great strength!

"Greater love has no one than this, that someone lay down his life for his friends."
John 15:13

Take turns praying and thanking God for His great love and for showing you how to share His love with others!

For more family fun, check out jellytelly.com, a partner for Christian parents.